Nate Likes to Skate

BRUCE DEGEN

I Like to Read®

Holiday House / New York

I LIKE TO READ is a registered trademark of Holiday House, Inc.

Copyright © 2016 by Bruce Degen
All Rights Reserved
HOLIDAY HOUSE is registered in the U.S. Patent and Trademark Office.
Printed and Bound in November 2015 at Tien Wah Press, Johor Bahru, Johor, Malaysia.
The artwork was created with graphite pencil and colored pencils
on Fabriano Artistico 140 lb. paper, soft press surface.
www.holidayhouse.com
First Edition
1 3 5 7 9 10 8 6 4 2

Library of Congress Cataloging-in-Publication Data
Degen, Bruce, author, illustrator.
Nate likes to skate / Bruce Degen. — First edition.
pages cm. — (I like to read)
Summary: A boy who likes to skate and a girl who likes
hats become friends, despite their differences.
ISBN 978-0-8234-3456-5 (hardcover)
[1. Stories in rhyme. 2. Friendship—Fiction.] I. Title.
PZ8.3.D364Nat 2016
[E]—dc23
2014048568

ISBN 978-0-8234-3543-2 (paperback)

For Dr. J. Malin, orthopedic surgeon:

I'd like to thank you, Dr. Joel,
A skillful, kind and thoughtful soul.
You fixed me up and made me whole;
I'd like to thank you, Dr. Joel.

Nate likes to skate.

Kate likes hats.

"Kate, do you skate?"
Nate says.
"It's great!"

Kate says, "No, Nate.
I hate to skate.
Do you like my hat?"

Nate says,
"I hate that hat.
It's a great big bat."

Kate takes it off.

Nate skates on a grate.

He falls flat.

"It's late," says Kate.
"Bye, Nate."

Nate says, "Wait, Kate.
Don't close the gate.
I was a brat.
Can I try your hat?"

Kate says,
"I was a brat too.
You can try my hat.
Can I try to skate?"

Nate says,
"This hat looks great."

Kate says, "Look, Nate!
I can skate. Wheeee!"

Now Nate and Kate skate . . .

and wear hats.

And it feels great.

ALSO BY BRUCE DEGEN

I Said, "Bed!"
an I Like to Read® Book

"Everything about this book is solid, from its picture-book size
to its seamless melding of story and art. It raises the bar
on what a beginning reader can be and will inspire
any child to enjoy reading."
—*School Library Journal*

"Simple speech bubbles drive this imaginative early reader."
—*The Horn Book Guide*

Snow Joke
an I Like to Read® Book

"Making great use of simple diction and concepts, a repetitive
refrain ('that's not funny'), and clearly drawn illustrations built
for visual learning, Degen presents a story that's not only
perfect for budding readers but also one that teaches
kindness and etiquette at an early age."
—*Booklist*

"Anti-social high jinx deliver a lesson in kindness
and in learning to read. . . . A snow book that
deserves a warm reception."
—*Kirkus Reviews*

"Readers will learn important lessons about
friendship and forgiveness. "
—*School Library Journal*